The Duck Who Played the Kazoo

by Amy E. Sklansky ◆ Illustrated by Tiphanie Beeke

Clarion Books ♪ New York

Clarion Books
a Houghton Mifflin Company imprint
215 Park Avenue South, New York, NY 10003
Text copyright © 2008 by Amy E. Sklansky
Illustrations copyright © 2008 by Tiphanie Beeke

The illustrations were executed in watercolor and mixed media.
The text was set in 20-point Italia Book.

www.clarionbooks.com

Printed in Singapore

Library of Congress Cataloging-in-Publication Data
Sklansky, Amy E.
The duck who played the kazoo / by Amy E. Sklansky ; illustrated by Tiphanie Beeke.
p. cm.
Summary: After a hurricane blows through and with only his kazoo for company,
a lonely duck searches for friends but soon realizes there is no place like home.
ISBN-13: 978-0-618-42854-0
ISBN-10: 0-618-42854-2
[1. Ducks—Fiction. 2. Stories in rhyme.] I. Beeke, Tiphanie, ill. II. Title.
PZ8.3.S6288Duc   2007
[E]—dc22   2006029204

TWP 10 9 8 7 6 5 4 3 2 1

For my Phoebe bird
          —A.E.S.

For Lydia and Sianna
with love and happiness
          —T.B.

There once was a duck
who loved the kazoo.
He played:

La ditty, da ditty
zu zu.

Rising each morning,
feathers damp with the dew,

he would paddle all day
on the lake that he knew.

Splish, splash.
Splish, splash.
Zu zu.

But he'd been all alone
since the hurricane blew,
his only companion
the shiny kazoo.

Lonely tunes.
Long afternoons.
Zu zu.

Soon the days grew shorter,
and the cold winds blew.

Br-r-reezy.
Fr-r-reezy.
Zu zu.

So the duck packed his things
and gazed at the view.
"Good-bye, my dear lake.
I'll truly miss you."

And he played a sad song
on his shiny kazoo:

*La ditty, da ditty
zu zu.*

In the rain and the sun
toward the south he flew,
till he spotted a river
and other ducks, too.

Heavy things.
Tired wings.
Zu zu.

"Hello!" called the duck.
"How do you do?
  Let me play you a song
  on my shiny kazoo."

Wings clapping.
Feet tapping.
Zu zu.

"Hooray!" they all shouted
when his tune was through.
"Would you like to swim
with our fine-feathered crew?"

"You bet.
Let's get wet!"
Zu zu.

They floated downriver,
two by two,
and came to a place
where water plants grew.

Bottoms up.
Time to sup.
Zu zu.

Then they paddled upriver
to check out the view,
quacking along
with his shiny kazoo:

La ditty, da ditty
zu zu.

But buds on the branches,
and longer days, too,
made the duck think of home
and the lake that he knew.

Deep pool.
So cool.
Zu zu.

"Excuse me, dear ducks,
I'd like to ask you
to come for a visit
to my lake so blue.

"Please come.
We'll have fun."
Zu zu.

His friends were excited
to see someplace new,
and spoke all at once,
"Yes, we'll fly there with you!"

Quack-quacking.
Busy packing.
Zu zu.

So they took to the sky
and off they all flew,
while the duck played this song
on his shiny kazoo:

*La ditty, da ditty
zu zu.*